The Berenstain Bears'®
BEDTIME BATTLE

Stan & Jan Berenstain

Reader's Digest Kids

Westport, Connecticut

It was eight by the clock,
and all around town,
the creatures of Bear Country
were all settling down.

The deer in the forest,
the squirrels in their trees,

the mice in their nests,
the birds and the bees.

Cousin Fred's pup,

Farmer Ben's sheep

were all settling down
for a quiet night's sleep.

But there was one place in Bear Country that was *not* quiet within.
It's where the great bedtime battle was about to begin.

The floor was covered
with toys of all sorts:
There were dinosaurs, cars,
cannons, and forts,

all kinds of dolls,

wearing all kinds of clothes.

There was even a doll

who could blow her own nose.

Then Mama came in.

She had a big box.

She stepped over dolls.

She stepped around blocks.

"Now hear this!"
Mama Bear said.
"It is eight by the clock!
It is time for bed!

"Here's bedtime rule one:
AT THE END OF THE DAY,
WE PICK IT ALL UP,
AND WE PUT IT AWAY."

Dinosaurs, puzzles,
dolls, trucks, and blocks—
all of them went
into the box.

"Here's bedtime rule two,"
Mama Bear said:

"UPSTAIRS YOU GO,

UPSTAIRS AND TO BED!"

"Piggyback, please!"
shouted Sister and Brother.
So upstairs they went
on the poor aching backs
of their father and mother.

Then Mama Bear said,
"I don't want to be mean.
But here is rule three:
WE GO TO BED CLEAN."

So off with their clothes,
and into the tub,
went Sister and Brother
for some scrub-a-dub-dub.

Then it was time
for the cubs' shampoo.
"Stop splashing!" shouted Papa.
"I'm getting wetter than *you!*"

"Part of clean," said Mama,
"is brushing your teeth—
the ones above,
the ones beneath.

"But please do not squeeze
the toothpaste so hard.
You need just an inch,
not a foot or a yard."

So the battle went on.
For, once it's begun,
the bears' bedtime battle
goes on till it's done.

Into their room
went Sister and Brother
with their wet and tired
father and mother.

Sis got her sleeper down off the shelf. She didn't want help. She could do it herself.

"Hmm. There's just one problem,"
said Sis with a frown.
"I've put on my sleeper
upside-down!"

"Now," said Mama,
"I have one rule more.
Listen, my dears,
to rule number four:

"AT BEDTIME IT'S PROPER
FOR GOOD LITTLE BEARS
TO KNEEL BY THEIR BED
AND SAY THEIR PRAYERS."

Bless Mama and Papa,
and Gramps and Gran,
the oldest members
of our clan.
Bless Auntie Min
and Uncle Ed,
and don't forget
our cousin Fred...

"Stop!" Mama cried.

"Those blessings of yours

may be very clever.

But here's my rule six:

YOU CAN'T PRAY FOREVER!"

It was storytime.

The bedtime battlers had had enough.

Sis chose *The Little Red Hen.*

Brother Bear chose
The Three Billy Goats Gruff.

As Papa Bear read,

he began to doze.

Then Mama Bear's eyes
began to close.

Who won the battle?
Was it Father and Mother?

As you can see,
it was won by none other
than wide-awake Sister
and wide-awake Brother.